Writing Builders

Isabella and Ivan Build an
INTERVIEW

by Ann Ingalls
illustrated by Melanie Siegel

Content Consultant
Jan Lacina, Ph.D.
College of Education
Texas Christian University

NORWOOD HOUSE PRESS
CHICAGO, ILLINOIS

Dedication: For my children, Sarah, Kevin, and Mary

Norwood House Press
P.O. Box 316598
Chicago, Illinois 60631
For information regarding Norwood House Press, please visit
our website at:
www.norwoodhousepress.com or call 866-565-2900.

Editor: Melissa York
Designer: Christa Schneider
Project Management: Red Line Editorial

Paperback ISBN: 978-1-60357-389-4

The Library of Congress has cataloged the original hardcover
edition with the following call number: 2011038968

Manufactured in the United States of America in North
Mankato, Minnesota.
195N—012012

Words in **black bold** are defined in the glossary.

Doing an Interview Is a Piece of Cake!

I know a lot about interviews. Three years ago I was adopted into a family with a girl my age. That girl, Isabella, is now my sister. By asking questions, we learned about each other.

I know that Isabella and I both like the color blue, we both like to ride bikes, and we both really like chocolate chip cookies.

When Mrs. Henton, our teacher, asked our class to interview people in our community, I was sure I could do a good job.

Choose the right person, set a time and a place for the interview, and do lots of research. That way we'll know which questions to ask. This should be a piece of cake!

By Ivan, age 10

Isabella and Ivan stopped at the Sweet on You Bakery on the way home from school. The bell on the door rang as they pushed it open. Mary, the owner, stood at the counter ready to take their order.

"The usual?" she asked.

The children looked at the cases. They were full of breads, rolls, pastries, muffins, cookies, scones, and all kinds of good things to eat.

"Yes, please! Two chocolate chip cookies and one blueberry muffin," said Isabella.

"Dad never gets tired of blueberry muffins," said Ivan.

"And we never get tired of chocolate chip cookies—or at least these chocolate chip cookies," said Isabella. "They're the best!"

"I think so too," agreed Mary.

"Why are these so much better?" asked Ivan. "What do you put in them?"

Before Mary could answer, Isabella remembered their school project. They had to **interview** someone in the community and write a report about what they learned. She realized Mary would be a perfect person to interview.

"I have an idea!" said Isabella. "Mary, may we meet with you for our school project? You would be our interviewee."

"Interviewee?" asked Mary. "You mean the person who is being interviewed, right?"

"Right!" said both children. "Let's make our plans," added Isabella.

"Sure! Can I wipe the sugar off my hands before the interview?" she laughed.

"Of course," replied Isabella.

"Remember, we need to pick a time that works best for Mary," added Ivan. "We don't have to do it today."

"That's right!" said Isabella. "Mary, when is a good time for you?"

"I usually have some time before the bakery opens. But I get to work at four o'clock in the morning," she said.

"Would you have time for an interview that early?" asked Ivan.

"Not right at four o'clock, but how about at six? I could take a short break, and you could have breakfast here with me."

"That would be so much fun!" said the children at the same time.

"Today is Monday. How about Thursday morning?"

"I'll check with Dad about giving us a ride and let you know tomorrow. Thanks, Mary!" said Isabella.

8" Cake 12.50
10" Cake 15.00
Custom cakes
✿ available ✿

During dinner they asked their father, Mr. Russo, if they could go to the Sweet on You Bakery on Thursday at six o'clock for an early interview.

"Only if I can get a cup of coffee with my blueberry muffin," he said.

"I'll call Mary to tell her that we'll be there bright and early," said Ivan. "I'm glad we made a plan."

"And we've got to go to the library to do some **research** on bakeries," said Isabella.

After school, Isabella and Ivan went to the library. Isabella checked out four books: two cookbooks and two books about bakeries.

When Ivan and Isabella got home, they sat down at the kitchen table. "Where do we start?" asked Ivan.

"Mrs. Henton said we need to think about what we want to learn from the interview, or what we want others to learn," answered Isabella.

"Then I'd like to learn about how the bakery works," said Ivan.

"That's perfect!" said Isabella. "Now we've got to write some interview questions."

"Mrs. Henton said the questions need to start with how, who, what, when, where, or why," added Ivan.

"Let's start with this," said Isabella, writing down her first question.

How long have you been in the bakery business?

"That's good," said Ivan. "How about this?"
He added some more questions quickly.

How did you come up with the name Sweet On You Bakery?

What's your favorite thing to bake?

He paused. "What about, 'Who are your favorite customers?'" asked Ivan with a smile.

"We can't ask that," said Isabella. "That doesn't give us any information about how the bakery works."

"Okay," said Ivan, "how about, 'What is the strangest thing you ever had to make?'"

"I think that's better," said Isabella. "I'm sure she's had to make lots of unusual cakes. And I wonder where she's had to take them."

Ivan wrote down two questions.

What is the strangest thing you ever had to make?

Where is the strangest place you've taken a cake?

Isabella asked, "What about this: 'Have you ever made applesauce muffins?'"

"But she could just say 'no.' We want more details than that," said Ivan. "How about, 'What kinds of muffins do you make?'"

Isabella clapped her hands. "Then we could ask, 'How do you decide what flavors to make?' Mrs. Henton called that a follow-up question, when you think of a new question based on the other person's answer."

The two filled the paper with the rest of their questions.

QUESTIONS

1. How long have you been in this business?
2. How did you come up with the name Sweet On You Bakery?
3. What's your favorite thing to bake?
4. ~~Who are your favorite customers?~~
4. What is the strangest thing you ever had to make?
5. Where is the strangest place you've taken a cake?
6. ~~Have you ever made applesauce muffins?~~
6. What kinds of muffins do you make?
A follow-up question could be: How do you decide what flavors to make?
7. Why do you get to the bakery so early each morning?
8. When do you close?
A follow-up question could be: What do you do to close up shop?
9. Who delivers the cakes?
A follow-up question could be: Has anyone ever dropped a cake?
10. How do you come up with new recipes?
11. What is the best thing about being in the bakery business?
12. What is your best-selling item?

When they were done writing questions, the two planned how they would **conduct** the interview.

"I think we should write down everything that Mary says, or we might forget something we need for our report. I don't want to just film the interview or record the sound. What if our batteries fail?" asked Ivan.

"Let's take our notebooks for the interview. If we each write down the questions and leave big spaces to write down the answers, we won't forget anything," said Isabella.

"We have to organize our notes from the interview afterwards. That way we can write our report," said Ivan.

On Thursday morning when the kids and Mr. Russo walked into the bakery, it was still dark outside but Mary was waiting.

"Don't forget, Ivan," said Isabella, "we have to let Mary do most of the talking."

"Let's go up to my office where it is quieter and we won't be distracted," said Mary. Several bakers in white aprons and caps were standing over noisy mixers, blending sweet batter. They had flour on their shirts and lots of it was sprinkled on a big marble counter.

"Go ahead and pick out something from the case, then follow me upstairs," instructed Mary.

Once they were all together in Mary's office, the children began to eat banana muffins. Then they took out their pencils and spiral notebooks. They opened their notebooks, where each had copied all the interview questions.

"Mary, thanks for agreeing to meet with us. Thanks for the muffins and juice, too," said Isabella. "First Ivan will ask a question and then I will, if that's all right."

"Sure thing," said Mary.

"This is going to be a piece of cake," said Ivan. "First question. How long have you been in this business?"

"My husband, Hank, grew up in the bakery business. It has been in his family for more than 50 years. Our son, Lincoln, wants to take over when we retire."

"How did you come up with the name for your bakery?" asked Isabella.

"That was easy," said Mary. "When Hank and I were dating, he said, 'I'm sweet on you.' That decided it. When we took over the bakery five years ago, we renamed it."

"What is the strangest thing you ever had to make?" asked Ivan.

"About two years ago, a lady wanted a wedding cake for her dogs. She wanted it to have dogs on top of the cake, and she wanted the cake to be safe for humans and for dogs to eat."

Ivan decided to ask some follow-up questions to learn more.

"How did that come out?" asked Ivan. "And how big was the cake?"

"I think she was very happy. The cake needed to serve 50 wedding guests."

"Did the dogs like the cake?" asked Isabella.

"I think so!" said Mary. "Many of the guests now buy baked goods for their dogs."

Ivan looked back down at their notes and asked the next question on the list. Mary answered while Isabella and Ivan took notes.

The two asked more questions than they thought they would. Mary's **comments** made them think of new things they wanted to know. Mary did most of the talking while Ivan and Isabella listened closely. Finally, they came to the last one on the list.

"What is your best-selling item?" asked Isabella.

"Bagels and muffins sell well, but chocolate chip cookies are our best-selling cookies," said Mary.

"Now that you mention chocolate chip cookies," asked Isabella, thinking of another follow-up question, "what is your secret ingredient?"

"Can you keep a secret?" asked Mary.

Ivan and Isabella both nodded their heads.

"We grind up pounds and pounds of oatmeal every day and add that to the batter. That makes the cookies lighter and tastier," said Mary.

When the interview was over, Ivan said, "Mary, here's our phone number. If you think of anything else, please call us."

"We're going home to write the report," added Isabella. "We have to read our notes and decide what information to include."

"When we finish writing the report of this interview, would you like a copy?" asked Ivan.

"I sure would," said Mary. "I'll put it on the bulletin board over by the coffee pot and orange juice to remind me of my favorite customers!"

You Can Do an Interview, Too!

THE INTERVIEW PROCESS

Making Plans

Think about who would be the best person to interview. Call, e-mail, or talk to the person you would like to interview to set up a time and place.

Decide how you will conduct the interview: in person, on the telephone, or by e-mail.

Preparations

Do research. Go to the library, look on the Internet, and ask people you know to provide background information.

Write 10 to 15 short, specific questions. Consider what follow-up questions you might want to ask.

Interview

Smile and use your best manners. Relax. Chat for a few minutes before the interview to put the interviewee at ease.

Take good notes. Otherwise, if your recording device fails you or your batteries die, that could be the end of your story.

Be a good listener. Give the interviewee time to answer. Do not interrupt or hurry responses. If the interviewee departs from your original questions, politely bring him or her back on topic.

At the end of the interview, ask if there is anything else he or she would like to say.

Thank the interviewee for his or her time. At the end of the interview, give your contact information to the interviewee so he or she can get in touch with you if they need to.

Report

As soon as possible after the interview, find a quiet place to read your handwritten notes. If you wait too long, you may forget what some of your notes mean.

Underline quotes that seem most important. Check that the answers are next to the correct questions.

Organize your notes, rewrite them in complete sentences, and write up your report.

Glossary

comments: statements or notes that tell an opinion.

conduct: to carry out an activity such as an interview.

interview: a meeting where one or more people ask questions of another to learn about that person.

research: to search for facts and information that you don't already know.

For More Information

Books

Frederick, Sara Gilbert. *Write Your Own Article: Newspaper, Magazine, Online*. Minneapolis, MN: Compass Point, 2009.

Guthrie, Donna, and Nancy Bentley. *Young Journalist's Book: How to Write and Produce Your Own Newspaper*. Brookfield, CT: Millbrook, 2000.

Websites

How to Conduct an Interview. http://www2.scholastic.com/browse/article.jsp?id=3752516

This website includes tips for conducting an interview.

How to Conduct an Interview. http://tutorgiant.com/tip_254.htm

Learn how to set up and conduct an interview at this website.

About the Author

Ann Ingalls has written more than 100 stories and poems for children of all ages as well as resource materials for parents and teachers. She was a teacher for many years and enjoyed that job. When she isn't writing she enjoys spending time with her family and friends, traveling, reading, knitting, and playing with her cats.